OPPRESSOR-OPPRESSED

AFRICAN - AMERICAN FICTION

MRS.S.S.SOUNDARYA

This book is dedicated to my father

Mr.S.P.Shanmugasundaram

whom i think about everyday

"His soul is on the raven's wing"...

Contents

Foreword

The dissertation was written for my Master of Philosophy in fiction with specilization in African-American Literature. The subject of the dissertation is related to Oppressor-Oppressed in African-American Culture. This is very fascinating research topic as it is a portrayal of the place of women in society.

Preface

"Peace doesnot mean just to stop wars,
but to stop oppression and injustice"
-Tawakkol Karman

Men and women all over the world, irrespective of their differences of nationality, race, religion, colour or government are governed by more or less the same feelings and passions. Hence the inequality existing amid the haves and encompass has not remained a matter of scholarly interest but over the years it has become everyone's concern. The problem of oppressor in the African-American context is very much live, causing the frustration. Equality and justice for all remains a dream only, as long as oppression exists in any form,hence the book is to portray the impact that slavery and racism had on real lives.

Acknowledgements

I would like to express my special thanks of gratitude to my HOD, Guide as well as my dear friend who gave me a golden opportunity to do this wonderful project on the topic "Oppressor-Oppressed in select novels of Alice Walker" who also helped me in doing a research. Secondly i would like to thank my Mother,my better half and my lovable daughter for their moral support.

THE OPPRESSOR-OPPRESSED IN THE SELECT NOVELS OF ALICE WALKER

Chapter I

INTRODUCTION

The reputation of a literary work need not rest on the portrayal of the author's inner landscape, his dreams or experiences, nor does it just rest on higher themes and characters. On the additional furnish a work which utilizes one's experiences, expectations, yearnings and dreams, doubts and dilemmas to look at the world in a different light with the intension of creating a better, more prosperous and more peaceful world stands a better chance of being accepted and acknowledged.

Such a work not only draws the attention of the people but it attains their approval and appreciation too. Most of the legends, irrespective of the language in which they have been written stand testimony to their deep concern for mankind and its betterment. Men and women all over the world, irrespective of their differences of nationality, race, religion, colour or government are governed by more or less the same feelings and passions.

Hence the inequality existing amid the haves and encompass has not remained a matter of scholarly interest but over the years it has become everyone's concern. Before three hundred years, civil war has started to get farmers from Africa. Because of poverty in their Country they moved America to work. That was the period of grown in share market. Black people were treated as slaves. Young Women were harassed, which results in domination.

Blacks were dominated by white. Many Political leaders like Abraham Lincoln and Martin Luther king started their revolution. Population of blacks was increased. During 1900's the slaveries were decreased. Government implemented many rules. Africans were developed in all the aspects except in Education, fought for equal rights and only fourty eight percentages were educated.

Many people wandered as uncivilized without proper food and shelter. During 1960's health issues spreader all over, women were abused and harassed by White. Americans started to neglect them because of their disease. Blacks were suffering commencing racial discrimination. Equality is a concept deeply embedded in American constitutional laws, and to use the words of John Franklin, "One either has it or does not have it"(ix- xi).The urge ,the demand of the African-American to be treated as an equal ,his quest for equality still remains a distant dream ,and a non-entity in the scheme of the great .It has remained a dream for more than three centuries ,it remained a dream on 28 August 1963 for Martin Luther King, representing some two hundred thousand Americans; it remained a dream for Rodney king, and perhaps it will remain for many more.

Though each generation of Americans right from the seventeenth century, have "sought to create a social order with "equity and justice, as they understood it" (3-4), extending the benefits of impartiality and integrity to the

African-American has always been elusive, as mentioned by Franklyn. The people who came to America with the intent of settling there, did not have much problem with the troublesome natives, nor did they have any problem with the other Europeans. They could accommodate themselves to each other. But such an accommodation was unthinkable with an African or an American. The twin acts of slavery and prejudice had debased the African-American and the degradation has remained operative for centuries.

Franklyn mentions with indignation that it is unfortunate that even the Declaration of Independence, "said nothing at all about the widespread practice of trading in human flesh and holding human beings is perpetual Bondage"(14-15).For those who were at the rudder of affairs, the African-American. The general view was that a black is a black and an inferior, whether he was a slave or a free man. The discrimination was Prevalent everywhere.

African -Americans were officially excluded from the militia, they were barred from testifying against white persons, they were taxed more heavily than the whites were prohibited from owning real estate. They suffered these "discriminations against them, not because they were not free but because they were not white"(21)as mentioned by Franklyn.

In 1790,a law was enacted limiting naturalization to white aliens. The Congress of 1792 also denied opportunity to thousands of Negroes who fought in the War of Independence, to be enrolled in the militia. The Congress of 1802 excluded the African-Americans from carrying the United States mail, thereby revealing a blatant mistrust of even those free African-Americans.

It is a historical fact that at time of establishing a government at the new capital at Washington, the authorities made certain that free African-Americans were not only excluded from participating in the affairs of the government but also they would be remained constantly of their degraded position. Various Congress right from through sixteenth made certain that the African-Americans though free were deprived "every semblance of parity within the legal and the political system"(26), states Franklyn. As late as 1810, even when slavery was dead or dying, racial equality did not exist. The places of congregation for prayer were no expectations either. This resentment of the presence of African-Americans, even in places of worship makes one wonder whether there were two Gods, one for the white and another for the American, in the format of possessions prepared exclusively by the white oppressor and excluding the oppressed African-American. This is why Franklyn speculates, "Whether the denial of equality to a group is more painful to its members than it is to an individual who is singled out for such dubious distinction"(29). However,it cannot be deprived of that the denial of equality was humiliating and painful to the oppressed individual as able-bodied as the oppressed group. It is again undeniable that very few even thought of treating the American-Americans as equals.

There was speculations among the whites whether the American-Americans who were free were to be treated as other free persons. The most prevalent and dominant view was that they should not be. In south, American-Americans were treated worse than the untouchables and in the North, they were an oppressed and unprivileged minority. In the opinion of Franklyn, "The revolutionary dream of equality of all people was deferred by necessity, as the founding Fathers saw it, of protecting the invisibility of property and maintaining a stable social order"(34).To be precise, equality was differed because “a man not only had to be free, but also white,in order to enjoy equality or even to aspire for it”(35),to quote Franklyn again. In the opinion of the whites, equality for all, could be a principle that could be accepted in mind and that slavery was a fixed evil which could not be eliminated. It was thought that emancipation would minimise the problems of the race but equality was impossible, it was underscored. While in the south the American-Americans were enslaved, in the North they were oppressed lot.

As an idea of equality seemed to take roots and flourish during the years 1820 to 1840, the women started speaking out again the numerous forms of discriminations they were subjected to by law, custom and tradition. The opinion expressed by Franklyn in this connection is noteworthy: In seeking to shatter behind the barriers against them, they joined The struggle against human bondage, against economic Discrimination of every kind, and against those institutions and Practices, such as the saloon, male suffrage, and property laws which added to the stresses between the sexes amid assorted module of society.(43) By the end of the nineteenth century and during the early years of twentieth century, the betrayal, the betrayal of American-American was total and complete.

The United States witnessed the worst display of racial arrogance, bigotry and in the end the conception of racial equality was in total disarray, while the order of white racial superiority had been more deeply entrenched. It was in 1902,that William E.B.Du Bois mentioned prophetically that the problem of the twentieth century America would be the predicament of the ‘Colourline’. During the first two decades of the twentieth century the dream of racial justice and equality had turned into a horrible nightmare. The statistics of crimes committed against the American-Americans and the injustice rendered to them stand testimony for this. In this connection, Franklyn states: Some twelve hundred Negroes were lynch in the decades ending in 1908..eight major and many minor race riots during the same period...an entire battalion of Negro soldiers dismissed by the president of the United States without a hearing and without honor for allegedly participating in a riot.(68) The whites were operating from a premise that equality could not be shared. They refused to realise that "Equality could not be shared, but it could not be divided in a line of attack that some would be more equal than others"(96),states Franklyn. The president's Commission on Civil Disorders described the situation as "two societies, one black white-separate and unqual", and no more testimony is required to stress the point that the American-American society remained unequal and oppressed as late as the seventies and eighties of the twentieth century.

Joel Kovel categories the historical phases of white racism as 'dominative' racism,' and 'metaracism'. He calls 'metaracism', "the racism of technocracy, in which racist coercion is carried out directly and metaracism was predicted to become the foremost mode of the later years of the twentieth century" (ix-vi).It is important to realise that racism involves the Deployment of violence and Kovel cautions that "it might be expected that its metamorphosis from human agencies would yield a violence ever more impersonal and exteriorized"(ix-vi). In 1969, America survived a decade of extraordinary racial conclusions. Fourteen years later, a profoundly racist structure continued in America revealing itself in the level of deep economic inequality between the whites and the American-

Americans. The main force of racist oppression was being administered impersonally, through cold savagery of economy. While referring to the unleashing of economic oppression on the hapless American-American by the oppressive forces, Kovel says: Therefore racist oppression occurs today through the seemingly automatic laws of the economic system. It is well known that behind the racist system is one of class oppression...Thus the policy pattern of dividing blacks from the poor whites and native Indians goes to the founding of the colonies.(ix-vi) The decline in economic conditions has led to a decline in health and other indicator of the eminence of living of the American-American. The wordlessness, a technical term used to denote unemployment has its cascading effect on the American-American. Brenner reported in New York Times, dated 24 October 1982: Each one percent rise in the unemployment rate is accompanied by a 2% increase in the mortality rate, a 5-6% increase in the homicides, a 5% increase in imprisonment, a 3-4% increase in first admission to mental hospitals, and about a 5%increase in infant mortality.

The later statistics on the effect is of unemployment on American-Americans is much more devastating and shocking. This wordlessness, the result of economic injustice and oppression leads to family disorganization, rootless and the inevitable, marked rise in criminalization. This is cited as one of the reasons for the inevitability forced on the African American by Kovel: "This becomes the signifier of their role in the racist order. In other words, about the third, of the black population are becoming simply invisible, but outlawed"(ix-vi).

In a Gallup poll held in 1980,there was a wide difference of opinion between the whites and the American-

Americans about the improvement in the superiority of life for the American-American minority. It ranged between a high of 75% in the opinion of the whites and a low of 25% in the opinion of the American-Americans. It is a sad comment on the affairs, happenings to the African-Americans that not much change has taken place during the attitude of the whites, especially the law enforcing authorities, towards those oppressed African Americans.

In 1982'the public safety commissioner, and three police officers, all white, were found not blameworthy by an all-white jury, of systematically torturing black prisoners. On 13 January 1983 the police played the role of judge and executioner, by executing a group of seven black cultists who had only two 38 caliber revolvers and a knife, and "all the seven were execute on the spot at least three by shots in the back or back of the head"(ix-vi) mentions Kovel.

The brutal attack by the white police officers on Rodney King, an unarmed African American motorist was video graphed by an amateur and the pictures telecast all over the world resulted in spontaneous repulsion and outrage. But the police officers were not found accountable by an all-white legal system, resulting in one of the worst carnages and riots witnessed during the nineties. These incidents underline the fact that "there is an excellent law on the books, but scarcely a means of enforcing it"(ix-vi) as mentioned by Kovel.

In the field of housing, about the treatment meted out to the African-Americans, the less said, the better, An example is starred City, where the impulse to provide with a "racially balanced "environment ran up against tremendous difficulties. The whites moved out of an area when they sensed that the African Americans were becoming a majority and this led the managers of starred City to the decision of pegging the portion of the African Americans approximately to 30-40%.The African Americans were held off the list, making sure that every qualified white family got preferential treatment. This in general violates the Fourteenth modification to the constitution as well as the Civil Rights Act of 1965.Thus racism and acts of oppression are practiced in the forename of antiracism. Kovel remarks, "Meditation through the psyche by elides to technocratic manipulation, but the result is still racist"(ix-vi),in this connection.

The reaction of the African American is natural, caused by the oppressive conditions described and such oppressive conditions continue to prevail in the American society. The oppressor's desire to split the world for the selfish purpose of domination leads to resentment and anger of the oppressed. According to Kovel," Racism itself is the tendency of a society to degrade and do violence to the people on the basis of race, and by whatever mediation may exit for the purpose"(ix-vi).

The expression of resentment and anger by the oppressed African- American varies from person to person and from group to group. However, their intention is to create awareness about the problems of the oppressed African American. This may be called the righteous indignation of the oppressed for the oppressive conditions willfully forced by the oppressor. The sensitive and creative African American artist uses his artistic expression to create a powerful impact on the minds of the readers about their oppressive conditions.

The novel emerge at a time when the African-Americans as a community were suffering and struggling to gain a foot-hold in social and political life. The violence against the African-Americans, barriers to their free and fair participation in society and nation's economy and the untrammeled spread of anti- African-American propaganda are all unashamedly over. The novels of Toni Morrison and Alice Walker become equally significant by representing the plight of African-American women and shockingly for them their tormentors and oppressors. The pain and agony caused by the oppressed African-American turned oppressor make an vital part of their novels. In the light of these, this project intends to study the "oppressor-oppressed Relationship in Walker's novel.

Alice Malsenior Walker (born February 9, 1944) is an American novelist, short story writer, poet, and activist. Walker wrote the verse of her first book of poems, Once, while she was studying in East Africa and during her senior year at Sarah Lawrence College. She took a brief time off from writing while working in Mississippi in the civil rights movement. Walker resumed her writing career when she joined Ms.magazine as an editor. In 1973, Walker and fellow Hurston scholar Charlotte D. Hunt discovered Zora Neal Hurston's unmarked grave in Ft. Pierce, Florida.

The women chipped in to buy a meek headstone for the gravesite. Walker's 1975 article "In Search of Zora Neale Hurston", published in Ms. magazine, helped renew interest in the work of this African-American writer and anthropologist. Walker was stirred by Hurston, whose work and life predisposed her subject matter. Walker occupies an eminent place among African American women writers. During one of her discussions on the "intimate male-female encounters" over social confrontations in the narratives of African- American women,Walker observes; Twentieth century black women writers all give the impression to be much More interested in black community, in intimate relationships, With the white world as a backdrop...here just has not been enough examination or enough application of findings to real problems in our day-to-day living. Black women continue to talk about intimate relations so that we can recognize what is happening when we see it, then maybe there will be some change in behavior on the division of men and women.

Butler – Evans states," A commitment to write the "authentic" lives of "real" Black people occupies textual space with an urgency to tell the specific stories of Black women Alice walker. Alice walker has stated her position as a writer in one of her of her interviews; distracted with the devout survival, the whole of my People.

But beyond that, I am dedicated to exploring the Oppressions, the insanities, the triumph of black Women... for me; black women are the most enthralling creations in the world. Walker feels that a commitment to writing – to be significant – must be combined with social and political activism. She feels that it is the responsibility of the artist to stay close enough to his/her people and "to be there whenever they need "such a presence. To fulfill her commitment Walker uses her narravive, grounded in racial history and focus on the histories of women of Africa ancestry.

Butler – Evans states; Generally covering four or more decades in her novels, Walker Evokes specific historical events and personages, and her Metaphorical and metonymical representations of the Experiences of Blacks as oppressed people reflect historical Consciousness. She is also concerned with the specific experience of Black women, a focus that demands a feminist genealogy.(125) Butler – Evans also stated that a "Walker makes use of a "peremptory Moment of a feminine-feminist counter discourse" (126)as a dominant texual activity and "These historical narratives, become signifiers of sexual difference" (126).

Walker traces the history of African-American women's creativity in her essays, though she writes of the civil rights Movement with unreserved approval in 1967, Alice Walker contends later the Civil Rights Movement continued to oppress women and hence disastrous in its assignment of human liberation. These positions taken by Walker indicate that she is more committed to her people than she is faithful to her earlier statement.

In adding together to publish her collected short stories and poetry in 1970, that year Walker published her first novel, *The Third Life of Grange Copeland.* It explores the life of Grange Copeland, a rude, careless sharecropper, husband and father. In 1976, Walker's second novel Meridian was published. Meridian is a "semi-autobiographical narrative based upon Walker's experience in the 1960, it is her demonstration on the social, racial, and sexual upheaval that the Civil Rights and Black Power era produced." (12)

The novel dealt with activist workers in the South during the civil rights movement; with events drawn closely parallel to some of Walker's own experiences. Afro American Woman writer Alice Walker is a novelist in English. Racial oppression, general violence, history and ancestry, Civil Rights Movement – all these form the sum total of her work.

It was Alice walker who coin the term 'Womanism', a form of black feminism that affricates and prefers women's culture, women's suppleness and women's might. 'Womanism' according to Alice Walker is hardly restricted; it is committed to endurance and fullness of entire people, male and female. Alice Walker is a feminist, she is the leading Afro-American women black feminist.

Alice Walker's black 'womanism' realization is characterized by sexual racial, cultural, national, economic and political consideration. Alice Walker deals with oppression, racism, and sexism in America. Alice Walker's dissection of women into three kinds, as "suspended" part of main stream'; and "awaken by political force" is relatable.

Some Afro-American and Indian Women are resigned to their pose, to the lack of understanding between them and their men ('suspended'); others question their lot but unable to break away walk out themselves ('part of mainstream'). The third phase is that of uprising. More Afro-American women than Indian women are able to absolutely define themselves; long periods of economic independence, survival of three women household, and fondness for a daughter in the family are conceivably causal factors for this materialization of the awaken black women.

Alice walker's works consist of poems, short stories, novels and biographies. These have listed below: Alice walker's once: Poems appeared in 1968: *The Third Life of Grange Copeland*, a novel was published in 1970:You can't keep A Good Woman Down: Stories appeared in 1971;Revolutionary Petunias and other Poems appeared in 1972;In Love and Trouble: Stories of Black Women appeared in 1973; Alice walker's The Life of Thomas Lodge was published in 1974; Langston Hughes, American poet was also published in the same year; Meridian, a novel appeared in 1976;Good Night, WillieLee, I'll see You in the morning: Poems got published in 1979 and later in 1984: *The Colour Purple*, a novel appeared in 1983;In search of our Mothers' Gardens: Womanist prose appeared in 1983;Horses Make a Landscape Look more beautiful: Poems got published in 1984; To Hell with dying appeared in 1988; Alice walker's living By the world: Selected writings,1973-1987 was also published in 1988;The Temple of my Familiar was published in 1989; Alice walker's Her Blue Body Everything we know: Earthling Poems,1965-1990 complete was published in 1991 and her Possessing the secret of joy appeared in 1992. Alice walker has edited a book on Zora Neale Hurston.

Contemporaries James Baldwin was a civil rights activist, writer and essayist. Born in 1924 (the grandson of a slave) in Harlem, Baldwin never knew his biological father but was adopted at a young age by his mother's husband. At 14, Baldwin began to preach in the Pentecostal Church.

Just three years later, at seventeen, he left Harlem and moved to Greenwich Village, a zone known for artist and writers. During this time, he began to write short stories and book reviews, seriously predisposed by the Harlem Renaissance movement. In 1948, Baldwin moved to Paris, a move many people deem he did as a response to the treatment of Black Americans.

In 1953, Baldwin wrote Go Tell it on the Mountain, a semi-autobiographical novel about growing up in Harlem. The novel tells the story of the character John Grimes' 14th birthday. In each section, we experience another character's thoughts and through them learn about the family's life in the South and their relationship with each other.

Since her first novel, The Bluest Eye, was published in 1970, Toni Morrison has become a vote of African American women. Born in Ohio in 1931, Morrison majored in English at Howard University and then completed her master's in 1955 at Cornell. In 1957, Morrison started to teach at Howard University, and she began to write her first novel.

After roving for a while, she finally settled in New York where she begin working as an editor. Maya Angelou was an American poet, memoirist, and civil rights activist. She published seven autobiographies, three books of essays, several books of poetry, and was credited with a list of plays, movies, and television shows across over 50 years. She received dozens of awards and more than fifty honorary degrees. Angelou is best known for her series of seven autobiographies, which spirit on her childhood and early adult experience.

The first, I Know Why the Caged Bird Sings (1969), tells of her life up to the age of 17 and brought her international gratitude and commendation. With the publication of "I Know Why the Caged Bird Sings", Angelou publicly discussed aspects of her personal life. She was respected as a spokesperson for black people and women, and her works have been considered a defense of black culture.

Alice Walker's novels are considered as enlightening novels *The Third Life of Grange Copeland*, The *Colour Purple* and Meridian. Her novels are about the violence within the black community in the profound south mainly by men against their own families. In *The Third Life of Grange Copeland* women were dominated by men even by her husband. Margaret in Third life of Grange Copeland is being abused and isolated and treated as slave by her husband. Likewise Mem is murdered by her husband. This shows the male domination and slavery.

Men are also so angry at their unfair position in society that they take it out their wives and children and then in turn blame it on their treatment at the hands of white people. In *The Colour Purple* Celie the protagonist of this novel is being raped by her step father after the bereavement of her mother. She is also physically abused by her husband and treated ill very badly. Though Women got their own freedom and self-esteem, they underwent domestic violence. Alice Walker portrays the sufferings and oppression of women in her novels. *The Third Life of Grange*

Copeland is a debut novel of Walker, which is published in 1970.This novel, is about Grange and his family. Black People in America were wandering for their identity and conflicting for their civil right. Walker fought for the equality of black people. Certainly the third life focuses on a black family the Copelands. It tells the history of three generations Grange, Brownfield and Ruth and in the process records the speech," imagination" and "fantasies" that constitute their collective consciousness. In this sense, the book looks forward to the more complicated structure of *The Colour Purple* in which Nettie's account of African ancestry, symbolized by the Olinkas is integrated with Celie's first-person letter/diary that includes a multigenerational chronicle of her parents, her own loves and tribulations' her children and stepchildren and her grand children. But The Third Life departs significantly from Walker's primary concern "with associations amid members of a black family."Although Grange lives his "first life" with his wife Margeret and his "third or final" Alice Walker distinguished two major themes strains in black fiction :the chronicle of a black family and the tale concerned primarily with racial confrontation. Her remarks are worth quoting since they suggest, in retrospect, the formal and political problems that she explored and tried to reconcile in her first novel, *The Third Life of Grange Copeland*(1970).Her words anticipate too the preoccupations of Meridian(1976) and especially *The Colour Purple* (1982)."It seem to me that black writing has suffered, because even black critics have unspecified that a book that deals with associations among member of a black family or flanked by a man and a woman is less important than one that has white people as a primary antagonist. The consequence of this is that is that many of our books by 'major 'writers tell us little about culture, history or future, imagination, fantasies of black people and a lot about isolated or limited encounters with a nonspecific white world"(202) Grange's life originated with Margret as an optimistic sharecropper. Their marital life failed because of the misunderstanding and frustration of the couple.

The feminist decisive banter focuses on the different types of females in Walker's work, the societal roles they break or are supposed to fulfill, the women's issues treated in Walker's work, and reactionary critiques to the criticism of male critics, specifically regarding *The Colour Purple.* The conversation of theme centers on four major subjects: the role of silence and speech in Grange, the description journey motif, the role of folklore and oral tradition, and the role of family and community.

Three of these major themes, silence and speech, the narrative journey and family and neighborhood are dealt with in the lives of Margaret, Josie, and Mem, but the majority of the thematic argument does not mention their association in these imperative themes. A greater part of critic, including some who could be consider feminist, imagine three female characters, Margaret, Josie, and Mem, are victims.

Reviews directly following the publication of the novel in 1970 focus on different themes than those highlighted by the larger thematic discussion that continues in the 1980s and 1990s. But the views on the female characters from these early reviews coincide with the treatment they have received more recently. One female reviewer, Josephine Hendin, believe that Grange is about the "exhaustion of love" and that the female characters are "fatalities of both whites and their own husbands" (5).

While a male commentator, Robert Coles, a few months later, in 1971, states that the novel is about "the directions a suffering people can take" (7). Neither mentions the consequence or deeds of these female characters. Grange exploited by his white owner which results in indebtedness. And his earnings were not sufficient enough to last. Blacks were treated ill by White community people.

They sucked the blood of black people for their welfare by exploiting their labours. Blacks were suffered only because of whites. Even their families get spoiled due to the psychological factor undergone by African Americans. Here in this novel Walker brings out the typical circumstance undergone by Grange.

He feels inadequacy and lost hope, drinks heavily started an illegal relationship with a prostitute, and abused his wife Margret and son Brownfield. She discusses the female characters as women who represent the universal issue of sexism. But, by stating that in Grange, Walker explore the "black man's search for self-worth" and that "the casualty of that search are the wives of Grange and Brownfield Copeland" (154), she allows the men to govern the text and she relegate the women to the unnamed role of victim.

Margaret a typical women, she lacks herself responsibility, which results in an illegal relationship with a White and bears a light skinned baby. According to Walker Margaret is characterized as women of coward and lacks herself responsibility, even she kills her own child and herself, does not bothered about the little boy Brownfield. She does not bear the abandon of her husband. Women should be bold enough to face the problems but here Margaret is referred as a coward. Peter Erickson highlights one of the many reasons that critics have not curved their focus to Margaret, Josie, or Mem.

Erickson claims that "the point of view is evenly dispersed among Brownfield, Ruth, and Grange" (12). This reader does not find any even distribution of point of view in the text; if anything Brownfield's point of view diminishes severely when Josie enters the novel, leaving his point of view radically uneven in assessment to Ruth and Grange.

But this claim does not account for the point of view given to Josie and Mem several times in the text. Other critics assert that Grange, Brownfield, and Ruth are the main characters. Gerri Bates sums up how the majority of critics view these three characters: Mem is "a victim of gender-role socialization," her husband, and white society; both Mem and Margaret are "defeated women"; and Josie is just a "minor character" who serves as an example of what a father's rejection can do (65).

These surface-level explorations of characterization lead critics to dismiss them as less important than any of the others. The feminist discussion often allows these critical claims to go unchallenged. The feminist critical exchange is mainly limited to Ruth; this indicates that another subject matter was depicted the consideration of feminist critics.

A major part of the discussion is animated and has demanded a great deal of attention from feminist critics defensive Walker's depiction of African American life. A part of the critical conversation is made up of chiefly black males who dislike and reject Walker's demonstration of black males in her novels. The feminist conversation in this realm consists of critics explaining the sources of the male reaction and the misreading that has led to those reactions.

The novel describes the lives of these women as they struggle with society, their landlords, and their husbands.

These women survive partially by taking on a role or behavior previously belonging to men. Unlike the others, Ruth has the opportunity for a life without male. Woman is a crucial part of society. No society or country can progress without the active contribution of women.

Although the place of women in society has changed from age to age and culture to culture, fact common to all societies is that a woman has never been considered equal to a man. She is treated as inferior and a second rate citizen. Her identity and status is derived from her relation to the gendered categories of mother, daughter, daughter-in-law and wife.

She is always definite not only in relation to man but as dependent on man and secondary to him. The discrimination begins right from her childhood as she is treated differently. Male superiority is inculcated in her.

The problem of oppressor in the African-American context is very much live, causing the frustration. Here the frustration of Women also pronounced by making them worst affected and exploited. Equality and justice for all remains a dream only, as long as oppression exists in any form. The aim of the study is to portray the impact that slavery and racism had on real lives.

2

Chapter II
THE OPPRESSOR-OPPRESSED

Alice Walker has distinguished the chronicle of an African - American family and the tale concerned primarily with racial confrontation as the two major strains of African – American fiction. Her remarks suggest that the formal and political problems she tried to reconcile in her first novel, Walker's *The Third life of Copeland* (1970) mentions Harold states, her words anticipate, too, the preoccupations of Meridian(1976) and especially *The Colour Purple*(1982)" (113-128) *The Third life of Copeland* focuses on an American family of Copelands and makes a record of its history covering three generations – Grange, Brownfield and Ruth. Her next novel Meridian reveals her conviction that oral expression is basic to building both personal and communal identity and Walker's *The Colour Purple* reveals through "Celie's letters to God Nettie,..her growing self-awareness and confidence as a sexual and capable woman"(113-128) The Third life reveals the conviction that even at one's death one can preserve what he values in life.Walker seems to have introduced through the phenomenon of willingness to die,one can continue to live through someone else. This continues in Meridian with Meridian Hill's only reason for self-sacrifice being the intention of preserving another life. *The Colour Purple* at its heart reveals a "complex redemptive artistry that encompasses saving gestures of various types"(437-451) mentions Felipe Smith.

An interview is held with Alice Walker, she stated that the reason behind writing this novel:"And I wanted to explore the relationship between men and women, and why women are always condemned for doing what men do as an expression of their masculinity. Being labelled as "gothic" is against her work. According to Walker her works should be related to the real life. *The Third Life of Grange Copeland* is a realistic plot.

She wants her readers to be able to differentiate the reality and unreality. Walker's vision projects the eyes of black female characters. Walker's was influenced by her family too because of that she wrote this novel. Domination is the only thing which is applicable to her family. Her father's need to dominate her mother and children, both physically and verbally. Her family embedded with violence.

Her father is considered as evil greedy men, he almost broke the courage of a strong woman, her mother. Walker points out that black woman in a world is dominated by white males. She is a black writer, compassion for the earth, a trust in humanity beyond our knowledge of evil, and an abiding love of justice.

We come into a great accountability as well, for we must give voice to centuries not only of silent unpleasantness and revulsion but also of neighbouring kindness and sustaining love. *The Third life of Copeland* portrays Walker's involvement about the society and the racist people. She focuses of the struggle of Black people, who try to claim their own lives, punishing against the barbed wired wall of racism, sexism, age, ignorance and despair.

Hence their struggles are endless. They were trapped and threaten by whites. The struggles and frustration of Blacks were well brought out by Walker in this novel. Her novels deals with everyday violence which is against her characters. Racial experience is narrated by Walker. The struggle which is portrayed in this novel exposes the inner and outer.

Walker the picture of the sufferings between the power of oppressive societial forces and the possibility for change. So Grange Copeland was expected to change. He was fortunate enough to be touched by love of something beyond himself, which changes his smothered and tense life. The Third life reveals the conviction that even at one's death one can preserve what he values in life.

Walker seems to have introduced through the phenomenon of willingness to die, one can continue to live through someone else. This continues in Meridian with Meridian Hill's only reason for self-sacrifice being the intention of preserving another life. *The Colour Purple* at its heart reveals a "complex redemptive artistry that encompasses saving gestures of various types"(437-451)mentions Felipe Smith.

The Third Life of Grange Copeland is obviously a novel telling the story of Copelands. It unfolds the history, the trials, death, defeats, oppressions and finally the hope of the three generations –Grange, Brownfield and Ruth. While Grange's and Brownfield's lives represent oppression and injustice, Ruth remnants a representation of hope and life.

In a way The Third life may be considered as a novel which states unequivocally that hope and life still flourish in spite of oppressions. The statement of James Butler: While Brownfield is a terrifying example of how the south can Physically enslave and spiritually cripple black people, Ruth's Story offers considerable hope because she is able to leave the South, rejecting the racist world which destroys Brownfields and,in so doing, move toward a larger, freer world which offers Her fresh possibilities.(194-204) Is worth mentioning here. Grange's life begins with Margret as an optimistic sharecropper.

Their marital life failed because of the frustration of the couple. Grange exploited by his white owner which results in indebtedness. And the earnings were not sufficient to survive. Blacks were treated ill by White community people. They suck the blood of black people for their welfare by the means of labours. Blacks were suffered only because of whites.

Even their families get due to the psychological factor undergone by African Americans. Here in this novel Walker brings out the typical circumstance undergone by Grange. He feels inadequacy and lost hope, drinks heavily started an illegal relationship with a prostitute, and abused his wife Margret and son Brownfield.

Alice Walker's *The Third Life of Grange Copeland* divided into eleven parts, running to forty-eight sections, commences with the impressions made during the childhood of Brownfield and ends with Brownfield being shot in a court of law by his father Grange, and Grange in turn shot in woods by the pursuing police force. Even at the beginning, the impressions made on Brownfield,reveal that such impressions are the result of oppressive conditions imposed on them: They told him (Brownfield) that his father worked for a Cracker And that the Cracker owned him..They told him that his Mother required to leave his father and go North to Philadelphia..They said that his mother wanted him, Brownfield,to go school, and that she was tried of his father And wanted to depart him in any case.

He thought his mother was like their dog in some Ways. She didn't have a thing to say that did not in some way Show her submission to his father. These impression made on the mind of a young Brownfield indicate the slave-like existence of Colelands. Being oppressor on his woman, treating her worse than a dog. Brownfield's mother works "all day pulling baits for ready money".

Brownfield remains undernourished and "When he was four he was covered with sores and pus ran from boils that under his armpits". Margaret was treated ill by her husband, she was longing for affection. She doesn't get much attention from her husband. She become distressed when her husband posses illegal affair. Grange failed to look after his family, he exposed his agony towards his son and wife.

Brownfield is conscious that "his father never looked at him or acknowledged him in any way". He is afraid of his father's silence and Brownfield's father had no smilies about him at all". A particular experience on an occasion when Brownfield is admonished – "say yes sir to Mr. Shipley" – makes Brownfield smell for the first time "an odor of sweat, fear and something indefinite". He tastes the total feeling of oppression, that his father might just be turned into insignificant dirt in the presence of the stranger.

Buthler-Evans comments, Brownfield's narrative concentrates all that is negative about Southern culture. He is cruelly persecuted by the excessive Racism and poverty of the Georgia wilds world in which He is born and raised...his is a case of wrecked growth; he is a Person who has been physically and emotionally withered by The nearly pathological environment which surrounds him.

By The end of the novel, he is portrayed as “a human being... Completely destroyed” (225) by the worst features of rural Southern life – ignorance, poverty, racism and violence.(194-204) Reveal the tragedy of Brownfield, mainly caused by the cruelties of racism, and oppression. During young age Brownfield suffered a lot, he felt unsecured.

The life of Copelands is full of uncertainties, following “a kind of cycle that depended almost totally on Grange's moods”. Then Grange abandons his family, driving his wife to position her young baby before committing suicide. Butler – Evans states the Grange “fails as a husband and a father”.

He mentions the following on Brownfield's failure: After being discarded by Grange and losing his mother shortly afterwards, Brownfield is frozen into a condition of southern servitude. His efforts to establish a new life fail..because his loss of family and the obliteration of self-esteem caused by a racist environment trap him in a kind of moral vacuum..

Literally cheated out of land and ethically expelled Of a human foundation for his life, Brownfield is satirically damned to repeat his father's failures.(194-204) One finds that the oppressed first life of Grange Copeland, leads to the Oppressive conditions of Brownfield's life gradually converting him another oppressor. While referring to the life oppression Grange, Hellenbrand states: Grange is propelled out of the south, and into self-awareness, By the oppressive circumstances of his first life.

Silence Characterizes Grange's oppression; punctuated by his own Unintelligible mumblings , it also signifies his resignation... Grange's first life is not one in which words or talk compensate For the abuse that he suffers in the world of work.(113-128) Hellenbrand states, "By implication, Grange is without a soul in his first life, since he is bereft of words and song.

Without spoken and shared community he must either flee or die"(113-128),thereby indicating that oppression not only makes Grange a silent, dumb animal, but also forces on him the limited options of flight or death. As mentioned earlier, Brownfield's behaviour results from oppressions he has undergone and in turn, converting him into a worse oppressor than Grange.

He was left alone his parents failed to care him and does not bothered about Brownfield. Even at his mother's funeral Brownfield can feel the shadows of oppression trying to overwhelm him. Though afraid to refuse the bait offered by Shipley, Brownfield reveals his contempt for Shipley, when he leaves the place."The fear of Shipley that had tied his tongue disappeared as the urge to sample his new freedom grew. He would be his own boss".

Brownfield marries Mem, and three years later is "in debt up his hat brim, 'Mem being "big with their second child" Soon Brownfield realizes that "his life was becoming a repetition of his father's". His debts grow year by year depressing him and he starts accusing Mem. He is determined to treat Mem "like a nigger and a whore". His crushed pride and his battered ego, his fume and his anger and his aggravation all combine in his ill-treatment of Mem.

He feels that cannot forgive his wife's greater knowledge. He beats his wife regularly, "trying to pin the blame for his failure on her by imprinting it on her face". The words of Hellenbrand, Sasistically,he wants her "to talk, but to talk like What she was, a hopeless nigger woman. Mem comes to speak like a verbal cripple. With love beaten out of her language, she sounds" like a tongue and trying to men from depression (57)".

Present a sad and realistic picture of the plight of the oppressed woman. Brownfield, an African American himself, finds pleasure in telling Mem that she is not white. By doing so he reveals that he is very much colour conscious. "Just remember you ain't white", he said, even while hating with all his heart the women he wanted and did not want his wife to imitate.

He liked to sling the precision of white women at her because Colour was something she could not change and as his own coloured skin exasperated him he meant for hers to humble her. Brownfield 's oppression makes Mem loose her dignity as a human being." she slogged along, ploddingly, like a cow herself, for the sake of the children. Her mildness became stupor; then her stupor became horror, desolation and at last, hatred". Grange returns, rejoins Joise and marries her.

Grange becomes very much attached to Ruth, his new-born granddaughter. He reveals his feeling of guilt for neglecting Brownfield by giving money and food to Brownfield 's family. Grange feels that the arrival of Ruth marks a new chapter."Laws knows the Whole business is something of a miraculous event. Out of all kinds of shit comes something clean, soft and sweet smelling".

Grange wandering and expressions at the North have made him more mellowed. Brownfield's ill-treatment of his wife worsens. Then Mem feels angry she remains powerless;"If was a man, she thought, frowning later. if I was a man I'd give every man in sight and that I ever met up with a beating ,maybe even chop up a few with my knife, they so pig-headed and mean"- Mem's feelings resembling Big Boy's fantasy of killing the whites. Mem manages to get a decent job and makes arrangements to move into a better house.

She feels," We might be a poor and black, but we ain't dumb. Atleast I ain't". She feels that she need not stand here and let this nigger spit in my face". She shows her determination to work harder and support her children. Only once in her entire life the oppressed Mem converts her anger against her oppressor into action, and that too after receiving terrible ill-treatment and beating.

While Brownfield is asleep, totally drunk, Mem picks up the gun, nudges the drunken Brownfield awake and resorts to teaching him a really good lesson. She tells him in no unsure terms her ten firm commandments, the last one being;"Youain't never going ugly nigger bitch can do when she gets mad" Brownfield is outwitted and out powered but he lays in wait for "return of Mem's weakness". He knows that "She was not evil and he would profit from it".

He manages to get Mem and children get evicted from their rented accommodation. Finally one night, Brownfield aims the gun" in his drunken accuracy" right into Mem's face and blows off her head. In Hellenbrand's words :Only in murder-of his own wife-does Brownfield believe that he has achieved" the power of the mobile, self-determined word"(166).

Brownfield , in other words cannot recognize what Grange learns: that his freedom depends on relation, not on isolated autonomy.(113-112) Brownfield gets sentenced for the murder of Mem, but his imprisonment does not reform him. Brownfield still remains an oppressor and he wants to get hold of Ruth, just for the sake of removing her from the protection of Grange.

Even while in prison, Brownfield continues" to plot evil". Grange voluntarily takes up the responsibility of bring up

Ruth, as his redemptive act. He reveals his angry reaction of the oppressed by telling Ruth about the White oppressors: "They story you from Africa." "They brought you here in chains." "They beat you every day in slavery and didn't feed you anything but weeds." "They did nasty things to women." "They are evil." "They are blue-eyed devils."

"They are your natural enemy." Grange feels," Besides such faith his acts against injustice seemed not just puny and ineffectual and selfish but cowardly as well". Grange can also distinguish the difference between physical and psychological oppressions; he has realized that from being recognized as a 'thing', he has been transformed to a non-existent state in the north; He was, perhaps, no longer regarded as merely a "thing"; what was even more cruel to him that to the people he met and passed daily he was not even in existence.

The south had made him miserable, with impudence ending raw from continual surveillance from contemptuous eyes, but they knew he was there... The North put him in solitary internment where he had to manufacture his own his tile stares in order to see himself. For why were they pretending he was not there? Each day he had to say his name to himself over and over again to shut out the silence.

The oppressive North has converted Grange into "a good theif", and beyond a few beatings "On suspiction" by the police", he has never been caught. His dreadful experience of trying to save a pregnant white woman from drowning and her contempt to accept the helping hand of a "nigger", makes him realize: The death of the woman was simple murder, and soul reproving; but in a strange way, a bizarre way, it liberate him..

It was the captivating of that white woman's life-and the Denying of the life of her child-the taking of her life, not the pleasing of her money that forced him to want to try to live again. He believed that, against his will, he had stumbled on the necessary act that black men must commit to regain or to manufacture their manhood, their self-respect. They must kill their oppressors.

This long passage reveals the strong reactions infused into Grange-during His second life at the North-the angry reaction of the oppressed, caused by the white oppressor. Grange feels that a new religion of 'hate', will make them survive;"Teach them to hate, if you wants them to survive" He feels that hatred for their oppressors will unite them, and the oppressed have to be taught hatred, while they are young; "Hatred for them will someday unite us",.."It will be the only Thing that can do it.

Deep in our hearts we hearts we hates them anyhow. If you teach it to them young, they won't have to learn it in the school of the hard knock". This hatred ,fighting with his oppressors and knocking them down also make Grange realize the futility of such actions, and the truth that each oppressed man must nave to free himself."Soon he realize he could not fight all the whites he met. Each man would have to free himself, he thought and the best way he could".

By this realization, Grange outgrows Ellison's Ras, the Exhorter. Grange has realized the true and bitter lesson that 'freedom' one has to earn money and be free."With his money..he bought a farm..He raised his own bread, fermented his own wine, cured his own meat. At last he was free". good sense in Brownfield: "..All I'm saying, Brownfield", said Grange, his voice sinking To a whisper, "is that one day I had to look back on my life and See where I went wrong..We guilty, Brownfield, and neither One of us is going to move a step in the accurate course until we admit it".

When all his efforts to save Ruth from the clutches of an incorrigible Brownfield fail,Grange shoots Brownfield in the court of 'law'.He tells the judge:"Iain' t running away .. I'm going home, and the first one of you crackers that visit me is going to get rest of what I got in this gun". He tells Ruth, "A man what'd do what I just did don't deserve to live. When you do something like that you give up your claim."

"Grange had not even left her the gun, knowing as she knew that she would live longer without it, at least in this battle". He does not preach violence to Ruth, but goes to the woods to be purchased and shot by the white police. Butler-Evans has the following to as on the novel's ending: As the novel draws to its close, Ruth, with Grange's help, Achievers her independence from her father and southern life in General..The novel ends on a painful note of ambivalence.

Southern bias erupts in violence which takes Grange's life' Yet his death frees Ruth for a new life of prolonged Possibilities...Walker, however, consciously avoids idealizing Grange's Southern home. As the novel's ending makes clear, it Is a small oasis of human love bounded by the same kind of Southern racial discrimination which has shattered the lives of scores of black people in the novel. Southern courts continues to take the lives of innocent people..(195-204) Hellenbrand 's observations are also significant in this context: While his first life is representative of black fathers and lovers Forced by futility to desert, Grange returns to family in his final incarnation..He returns with worldliness and expressiveness as well as love.

He has outlasted criminality, racial hatred and of course his original despairs and silence. This sequence suggests a painful lesson: not just that past cannot be escaped but, more relevantly, that white hegemony corner blacks into internecine conflict. The love story, the family chronicle, is distorted by the inexorable pressures of the white power.(113-128) The novel also reveals another aspect of a relationship, where the oppressed realizes a sense of freedom through acts of violence and killing as seen earlier in the case of Bigger Thomas, but giving the oppressed the ultimate realization that they must accept dependability for their actions, and they will have to help themselves to overcome their oppressors and ultimately the ugly oppression and injustice.

Pointing to repetitions and cycles in the characters lives in The Third Life does not take us far afield from the theme of silence. For Walkers wants readers' far afield from the theme of silence. For Walker wants us to sense that silence symbolizes those moments in her characters biological and emotional lives-especially, though not exclusively, her women's when they are most vulnerable to physical penetration and psychological manipulation.

Indeed Walker has said that although *The Third Life of Grange Copeland* is "ostensibly about a man and his son, it is the women and how they are treated that Colours everything" (Gardens 250-51) Brownfield's sense of self-worth as a black man is displaced for example both a dream of white wealth and his real submission to the crackers orders. While dreaming while submitting he is Walker tells us blankly "quiet".

He is, she observes," possessed" and filled by the images and imperatives of other (18).Such possession is symbolized poignantly in Josie's recurrent dream. Degraded by her preacher father for getting pregnant, unable to make him love her and speak to her, suffers nightmares in which he "rode" her "drenching her in perspiration., holding her immobile with weight"(38);she is "possessed" by a demon/ father who, quite possibly, possesses her sexually in the dream Brownfield lived with a father who was in a sense, possessed and haunted not by dreams but by the life that he actually lived.

As a child, his family's "life followed a kind of cycle that depended almost totally on grange's mood'(11).During the course of a week Grange terrorized his family through periods of respectively, moroseness, drunkenness and repentance. When silent, Grange was filled by whites commands or overcome by his own powerlessness.

Late in the novel, Grange explicitly invests the symbolism of biological periods with the theme of psychological vulnerability. He admonishes his son, "I'm talking to you, Brownfield, and most of what I'm saying is you got to hold tight a place in you where can't come"(209).The implication is clear..Grange, now older and wise, believes that his son, like himself as a young man, is controlled impregnate really by meaning ex-images fill Brownfield's silence, which illuminates Grange's effort to build a "sanctuary," a protected place for Ruth and himself when he returns from the North.

Impregnation applies, of course, only metaphorically to Brownfield's and vulnerability and to Grange's "kind of cycle" as a young man(11)But impregnation literally determines the fate of the women in the book. Josie's pregnancy alienates her from her father's love in turn; she is disturbed by dreams of her father's riding her. Grange's wife Margaret dies with her" bustard child" in her arms his departure. And Brownfield cruelly lies "in wait for the return of Mem's weakness.

The cycles of her months and years brought it. Her body would do to her what he could not, without the support of his former bravado"(101).When she is pregnant and unable to sustain her rebellion against Brownfield he beats her and forces her to move to Mr J.L'S place. He returns his family to the despair of cropping, for there at least, he is their boss. Later when Ruth begins to have periods."

She felt her Woman's body made her defenseless . She felt it could now be had and made to conceive something she didn't want against her will and her mind could do nothing to stop it"(193) These fears of defenselessness ,specifically of being "made to conceive against her will and her mind," suggest the link between biological and psychological impregnation.

Both body and mind can be forced to "conceive," can be in a word, raped as Grange implies to Brownfield, as Josie's life and nightmares dramatize an as Mem's return to submission displays. Meridian and Celie show a similar vulnerability to sexual and psychological manipulation, especially by men, before they build sanctuaries where others "can't come,".

Symbolically, then, it is no mishap that Grange believes that he kills a pregnant white woman, " A great blonde pregnant deified cow," in New York. The death compensates, in part, for his wife's suicide and murder of her child-two whites for two blacks to put matters crudely. Concurrently, he kills pregnancy itself, strikes out against the biological vulnerability which characterizes his own victimization as a black man.

This, the family chronic of walker's novel turns on an episode of racial confrontation. Grange's action launches him out of silence, passivity, and flight. Like Ellison's Ras the Destroyer, he begins to preach hatred of whites on the street corners of Harlem, through he comes to realize that such hate his futile. He cannot combat all the whites in the world, soon return south to construct an " inviolate" life. The scene of murder reveals Walker reworking, to her own ends, important episodes in Richard Wright's fiction and political psychology.

The pregnancy /vulnerability theme is hers even the white woman that Grange let's down as been betrayed by a soldier lover who uses money and a ring in a attempt to buy her acceptance of his leaving, but the characters and setting, even the lesson that Grange draws from the woman's death, bring to mind black/white collisions in Richard Wright's Native son and "Big Boy leaves Home". Walker's account of what, partially, she was trying to accomplish in The Third Life echoes Wright's comments on his compulsion to tell Bigger's tale in gripping visual detail:"I wanted, " Walker has said, for the novel "to be absolutely visual very real. It didn't want there to be any evasion on the part of the reader.

"she adds that she "know [s] many Brownfields".(Tate interview 176-77). According to Wright, in "How 'Bigger' was born," " where possible I told of Bigger's life in close-up slow-motion, for I wanted the reader to feel that there was nothing between him and Bigger; that the story was a special premiere given in his own private theater".(xxxii). And for Wright, "There was not just one Bigger, but many of them..." (viii). However, it is in Grange Copeland, during his first life, not in Brownfield, we can discern most clearly some of Bigger's Thomas's lineaments-his stuttering attempts to speak, his pent-up rage- even though, unlike Bigger, Grange eventually discovers his own voice and protects a loved one with it.

Bigger's voice is usurped by Boris Max, Who speaks only to the white world. In The process, he suppress Bigger's Mary Dalton, largerly as a "physiological and psychological reaction"(Native Son 355).Like young Grange, Bigger is an isolated in the middle of family. Bigger we're told, shut his family's "voices out of his mind.

He hated his family because he knew that they were suffering and that he was powerless to help them"(9),Also like Grange, Biger is trapped by "his swiftly changing moods," by" period of abstract menacing and periods of extreme desire: moments of silence and moments of anger"(24-25).And he, too, is peculiarly proud of his anger silence and moments of anger since it, at least, is his personal response to despair.

After his liberating murder, Bigger briefly becomes a storyteller. And he murders again, killing Bessie because she can only slow his efforts to escape his white pursuers. But before her death, he has conceived of her as an instrument in his plan to extort ransoms money from the Daltons.

He constructs a case against Jan to mislead detective Britten, and he becomes "giddy" with power when he imagines and writes a ransom note (151).For one Bigger seems to be plotting the story of his life .After murder, Grange also moves out of silence and into storytelling. However, he cannot bring himself to recount his murder to his granddaughter Ruth when she asks teasingly, " " tell me something real mean that you did " " (143).

He fears that his revelation of the murder and the hate that both caused hid and flowed from it would destroy Ruth's innocence and contaminate their love. "Hate left a man shamed, as he was now, before the trust and faith of the young." Moreover, he reasons that ". . . he could only teach hate by inspiring it , " and hate is the last thing he wishes to beget in his granddaughter (157).

Yet Grange does not wish to leave Ruth unarmed in a dangerous world. With a few significant differences, his behavior towards her parallels Nanny always " ' wanted to preach a great sermon about Coloured women Sittin' on high' " (31-32), but she lacked the pulpit. She could never take the "high ground" because she had to spend so much of her life scraping to make ends meet up sweating to raise her granddaughter.

According to Houston Baker, " . . . Nanny conflates the securing of property with effective expression. . . . Having been denied a say in her own fate because she was properly she assumes that only property enables expression" (57). Thus she advises Janie to marry Logan. While Grange does not advise his granddaughter to accept a rich old man, he does deliver a text to Ruth, not just after he has murdered, but after he has also secured property and finances for himself and for her.

He has returned south with a portion of the white woman's money, added Josie's funds from the Dew Drop Inn, and made enough money gambling to send Ruth through college. Murder, liquor, prostitution, and cardsharping provide Grange and Ruth with a stake for self-expression like that for which Nanny, escape silence and enter the world of individuation partly by capitalizing on the scant "goods" that he can gather in a world dominated by whites.

Grange's stories and talk are barbed with the insights of a man who has been constantly at odds with the law and the social structures of both white and black communities. Grange knows all the (122). "John" stories and frequently invents new ones. "John became Ruth's hero because he could talk himself out of any situation and remained her of Grange" (128 my emphasis).

Also, he tells Ruth the Uncle Remus stories but makes clear that he "thought that Uncle Remus was a fool. Because if he was so smart that he could make animals smart too, then why the hell . . . didn't he dump the little white boy (or tie him up and hold him for ransom)" (129).

Irreverently he compares the "Holy Ghost" with a "chill" and warms Ruth that, if she doesn't watch out, it could "turn into the soul's" pneumonia" (129). He also tells her of his being "saved" one hot day in church he bargained with God that, if a fly buzzed into his Uncle Buster's snoring mouth, he would go to the altar. Uncle Buster swallowed the fly, and that's the way that Grange got religion (130-32).

Obviously, Grange's sarcasm whittles away at the complacent values of his culture, although he does not want Ruth to reject her blackness. His desire is that she cherish only what is hard and truly alive, what is valuable for surviving in a world that to his eyes, does not differ much from John's "plantation" (128).

To drive home the historical evil of white power, he tells her that whites made blacks eat "'weeds' " (138) and that white folks are " 'the reason fences were invented' " –Indians never " ' done , hogged property from one another' " (175). Finally he "recite[s] from memory speeches, . . .newscasts, [and] lectures" that tell Ruth what her school books do not say: Whites stole her people from Africa, chained them, and enslaved them in America (138).

Grange is a rebellious storyteller, a cultural and historical revisionist who enlivens his discourage with sardonic analogies (the Holy Ghost as a "chill, " a sickness). Apt overstatement (whites made blacks eat "weeds"). And pointed parables ("fences" were because whites were "propity" hogs). He speaks an ironic dialect that signals his departure from the cultural norms that Ruth learns in school.

Much of the lesson takes, for Ruth objects to the childish prose and insulting diagrams in her school book that picture blacks as primitive creatures to the jungle. And she detects something dead, something senseless, in her teacher Mrs. Grayson, who "mounted all the words in the textbooks but they did not come out coherently as they appeared on the page" (184).

Grange, above all, conceives of himself as a teacher who can install racial pride and individual identity in Ruth. Then, perhaps she can be saved from self-hate and helplessness. Grange's lively critique does not drive Ruth from institutional learning forever, although occasionally she does hurl "Grange inherited words" at a foolish teacher (187) not is he tempted to pull (123). Her out, Not does she speak like him. Implied is a subtle dialectic in which Ruth, a young woman of learning.

Recovers her mother Mem's identity through the collision of Grange's agency and school for Mem taught school and sang songs of love to her husband Ruth comes to possess Grange's wit, hi critical faculty, as well as her mother's capacity for infusing "ABC's" and proper words with love (46). Indeed, Grange and Ruth mainly because they are two generations apart, nurture a love that is free from the lacerations of sexuality and even immediate family that scar the characters in so much of Walker's fiction.

Think of Grange and Margaret Brownfield and mem: of meridian and her stepfather, and Eddie, and meridian and Albert before their reconciliation in friendship. Wedded here is experience and innocence: until the end they learn from each other without exacting pain. When they dance together and Ruth's young body presses plainly against Grange's, there is no hint of perversity.

In dance she learns the "untaught history" of her race. Dance reincarnates, perhaps, her dead mother's music as well "dancing" Walker writes, "was a warm electricity that stretched, connecting them with other dancers moving across the seas" (134).

It is a form of inherited song, a ritual expression that unites the present with the past that lies beyond the Atlantic and beyond the grave. Arguably, Grange whose conversion to responsibility and love flows miraculously out of murder and Hate is the wish fulfillment of Walker's feminist consciousness. While his first life is representative of Black fathers and lovers forced by futility to desert, Grange returns to family in his final incarnation.

And he returns with worldliness and expressiveness as well as love. He has outlasted criminality racial hatred, and of course his Original Despair and silence. Thus his experience as a character brings together the story of familial feeling and the encounter of black versus white that Walker has identified as the often divergent streams in black fiction. But Grange's return does not close successfully.

The pain of his first life and the violence of his second come back to Haunt him in his third. Jealous of Grange's solicitude for Ruth and hungry for the money that Grange has bequeathed to her Brownfield struggles to get his daughter back. He runs to Judge Harry, who obviously enjoys playing God to blacks who shuffle and say "shucks" appropriately, and he convinces " ' justice' " to return Ruth to him (246). Grange will not hear of this. He shoots his son and brings the white law down on himself.

When viewed with Grange as the central figure, this Sequence Suggest a painful lesson: not just that the past cannot be escaped (124). But, more relevantly, that white hegemony corners blacks into internecine conflict. The love story, the family chronicle in other words, is distorted by the inexorable pressures of white power when we view Ruth as the central figure in this episode; however, a different configuration emerges. She is not trapped by the past Rather. With her father and grandfather dead, Ruth is left alone to face the future.

Grange's effort to protect her on the "sanctuary" of his farm has failed. Or has it? Grange has transmitted to her a legacy of cultural and historical stories: she has, too, his wealth to fund her schooling. And she has seen her grandfather kill, not out of hate, as he had before, but out of love-for her, Grange knowing that one day Ruth would have to ventures out on her own, had already recognized the blooming of her sexual feeling for a young man (237,242).

Perhaps, then he did not fail Ruth but, instead, freed her, while instilling her with a sense of past and of the cost of love. Certainly, The Third of Grange Copeland centers on a man Grange and dramatizes the convergence of racial antagonism and familial history in his life, his life, But in Ruth's fate. Even in the recurrent metaphors of period pregnancy, the novel pints towards the Walker's preoccupations in meridian and *The Colour purple.*

Indeed, in retrospect. The Third life appears to prepare for Meridian in the same way that Grange prepares Ruth. Ruth learns from Grange that love sometimes requires killing Like Meridian. If Ruth still is not sure whether or not she can kill. She learns the circumstances under which killing is understandable: the imminent violation of love or a loved one.

While Meridian is a lone heroine of the civil Rights Era, she, like Ruth, is removed from family but profoundly united to her cultural past. And Grange and current events (it is the Era of Civil Rights marchers) prepare Ruth to move into the world of politics, education, and womanly independence that Meridian occupies. Meridian does indeed appear, as Bettye J. Parker-Smith has suggested, "an extension of Ruth, who symbolizes some ray of hope at the end" (488). Ruth sees only Grange's strengths in this, his Third life before she is left alone. But we, through Walker's narrative, see his weaknesses as well-silence in his first life, hatred in his second. It is as if Walker views Grange Copeland, the first and last, male character central to one of her novels, with deep ambivalence-with respect for his capacity to grow but with sorrow for the selfishness and hate before moving on to female protagonists like Meridian and Celie.

He is, curiously, a transitional figure: looking back to Bigger Thomas. (125). Alice Walker's On Black Women Alice Walker contends that "Black Women now offer varied, live models of how it is probable to live. We have made a new place to move" (Washington 1979:146).

However, the Afro-American women, like the Indian women turn to their children for emotional accomplishment and companionship; to be able, without fear of disapproval which they often receive from their husbands, to talk, to laugh and to feel. Motherhood not only gives them satisfaction, but also power, even if lop-sided, which they lack in their marital relationship. The creature sparks of the survival culture of the 'suspended' black women is the theme in Meridian. The theme finds an apposite expression in the character of Meridian.

Meridian, to commence with, is a lonely, passionate Woman who has been physically and psychologically abused. But unlike the women characters in *The Third Life of Grange Copeland*, Meridian is provided with an opportunity to liberate herself, through the Civil Rights Movement. Initially she involves herself in a movement fully.

But as the Movement turns into violent revolution, she questions the authority of the violent means to achieve innovatory ends. She gains a sense of perspective and proportion through suffering, which she believes is essential to human development. The oppression which destroys all the imaginative sparks of Margaret and Mem, makes Meridian philosophical, as she imbibe the collective wisdom of her people Alice Walker fights the myth of the Black motherhood as a stereotype of strength, self-abnegation and sacrifice.

Margaret and Mem are harmed mothers shaped by the sharecropping system. Their idea of motherhood, gauge not stereotypical, is preventive. Mem's attempt at providing a good and defensive motherhood to Ruth fails, and the role is lastly taken on by George Copeland. Meridian's idea of motherhood is not preventive: 'she is torn between her own personal desire to become a mother and the fact that parenthood seems to cut her off from the possibilities of life and love' (AW, 64-65).

It is this contradiction in her desire which precipitates her quest to become another not in the biological sense of term, but in the philosophical sense when she takes to non-violent resistance for the sake of children. The repudiation of her cell, her sleeping bag and her role conceded over to Truman, again, is symbolic of the role of the mother earth that she had played.

Truman climbs untidily into Meridian's bag and realize the terror of the role of mother earth that he now has to play. She consequently passes on the struggle to guard life to Truman in order to understand the blessedness of life fully, symbolizing the beginning of the spirit, and also the beginning of another individual search. The novel is thus used as a meditative and methodical tool.

Women writers whether post colonial or not, comprise always been marginalized and excluded from literary canon. In a male subjugated value system, their work has been undervalued. Alice Walker, best known as the author of *The Colour Purple* vividly depicts sexism, racism, oppression and poverty parapet in life.

Her Pulitzer Prize appealing novel *The Colour Purple* deals with the struggle, both in America and in Africa, of women to gain appreciation as individuals who have a self and identity of their own, there by defying the manipulative and oppressive chains of a society dominated and constructed by male. All the women characters in the novel exhibits the determination of overcoming all kinds of oppression leveled upon them in order to live a meaningful life.

Alice Walker's *The Colour Purple*, is another novel, which has elicited both a wide range of praise and censure. Philip M.Royster considers a *The Colour Purple* a depiction of violent black men who physically and psychological use their wives and children"(347-370) In the words of Charles L.Proudfit, ...over an extended period of time,(the novel) enables Celie- A depressed survivor-victim of parent loss, emotional and Physical neglect, rape, incest, trauma, and spousal abuse-to resume her arrest development and continue developmental Processes that were disenchanted in childhood and adolescence.(12-37) To be precise, *The*

*Colour Purple*is a novel that explores the exploitation of the oppressed woman, the exploitation, abuse and harassment commencing from childhood, leading to traumatic experiences and leaving psychic scars in the victim. In Celie's experience destructive patriarchal power is associated with god. James C .Hall mentions: Celie's path to selfhood involves the evaporation of patriarchal Christianity... Her husband ... is also unnameable.

This textual Deletion signifies her "partner's" absolute distance, his inability to comprehend her history and future. He perceives her as Livestock, and denies her not only love but humanity. (89-98) Celie's husband not only ill-treats her, but he also makes advances on Nettie, Celie's sister.

For protecting Nettie, Celie must endure the indignities of her life. On the additional hand "Nettie's experience in colonial Africa, . . . further unravels the ties between institutional Christianity and black oppression" (89-98) states Hall. Alphonso's rape of Celie, and his using her as a sexual replacement for his exhausted wife is, "a not uncommon situation in actual cases of father-daughter incest" (47-49) according to Herman. It is kind of "soul murder".

It is actually through the "female bonding" with Shug, that Celie is able to verbalise her feeling about Albert, to realise her own adult sexual orientation and gender identity. It is through this female-bonding "Celie discovers that she has a creative and unique talent . . . she establish her own cloths business . . . and thereby achieves economic independence" (12-37) states proudfit. The words of proud fit are used to conclude this short discussion of *The Colour Purple*. In one of her essays, Living By the word, walker has remarked "there is no story more to me personally than one in which one woman saves the life of another, and save herself...", a feat that "black women wish they were able to do all the time".

The Colour Purple reveals the saving gestures of various types, the saving gesture offered by one oppressed victim to another, fellow oppressed. Without this saving gesture, Celie's life might have become a veritable hell, and it is this saving gesture extended by Celie – a victim of oppression herself-that make Celie serve as a maid and protector of her younger sister Nettie against the sexual advance of Alphonso. Celie comes to learn that, when she was barely two years old, her father's successful store and blacksmith shop were burned and destroyed; he and his two brothers were dragged from their homes and hanged by the jealous whites, and as her mother gave birth to Nettie, her husband's mutilated and burned body was brought home, which in turn led to an emotional breakdown of Celie's mother. "Although the widow's body recovered, her mind was never the same". Celie also learns that a single catastrophic evening made her suffer several losses; she lost her father, she lost emotionally her mother, she lost safety and warmth of a family environment, and lost her place as an merely child of the family.

All these losses dumped all on a sudden on Celie make her life miserable right from the beginning, paving the way for her exploitation and oppression by every opportunistic, odd and sundry oppressor. Alice Walker express about the black woman's struggle for equal rights. Racial discrimination and sexual politics were still exploring. These issues were taken by Walker and fought for the equality of women. In Georgia she was worked for civil rights project in Mississippi.

Her novels concentrated on black women and her sufferings. She was struggled for the wholeness and equality of women. Black people were treated brutally as slaves. Walker portrays the experience and culture of Afro-American Women and their oppression. It deals with the role of male domination in daunting black women's struggle for identity, subsistence, sovereignty.

Women are oppressed and humiliated and this novel shows how women's power is taken. *The Colour Purple* is considered as women novel it is about the tradition of black. The whole novel is about the protagonist Celie whose letters were written in series form. Initially Celie write the letters to "God" and latter to her sister Nettie, as well as Nettie's letter to Celie.

The plot begins in Georgia where the author narrates about the fourteen year old girl. Celie lives with her sister Nettie, where she was abused. Celie was tortured by her father Alphonso, whom she thinks as her father. Later she recognize that Alphonso was her step father. Celie cares for other children and done all the household duties.

She is denied to go to school, since according to her stepfather, she is 'too dumb to keep going to school'(Cp 9). Celie is physicaly harassed and abused by Alphonso. Twice she becomes pregnant and her babies were taken from her. Celie got two children, for the sake of money, both her children were sold by Alphonso. Celie'slife become worse than before even her Children were forcefully taken from her for financial benefit.

To overcome from the psychological torture she sent letters to God and Nettie. To Celie writing letters are like sharing her sufferings. Celie is totally stressed and heartbroken because of her step father, she feels her appearance becomes worst than before, she accepts that she is ugly now. Celie becomes a slave to Albert and a step mother to his children.

Celie wants to help her sister Nettie, when Alphonso was forced Nettie to come for living with Celie. She wants to protect her sister from her father and society. For that she have to be fit physically and emotionally fit. Walker brings out the fact of reality which is happening in the life of black women. Here she is telling about the pathetic situation of Celie who is forced to marry a man who is already married.

Celie is abandon by her step father, later she is abandon by a man whom she is forcefully married with her father's wish. She spends much of her life under cruel men. Hence Walker brings out the sufferings of Celie, which she faces during her life time. Celie's only relief is Shug, who teaches Celie about life and love. Walker portrays some suspense in this novel that Nettie's ship sinks when Nettie is resting on her way home from Africa. The suspense reveals about the sisters were reunited or not. After the long years of survival Celie's abandonment were come to the end.

Nettie returned home to meet her sister, and she brought Celie's children which the couple Samuel and Corrine bought from Alphonso. Samuel married Nettie after the death of Corrine. Celie was much worried about her children Olivia and Adam, now that worries also came to an end by the arrival of Nettie and her family from Africa.

The novel ends by the life of Celie and other characters keeps getting better. Celie recognise the value of life and learnt about self respect and self -esteem by the way she lived her life. Celie got a bitter experience in her life. She failed to possess a better life from the beginning even at the age of fourteen she was under control of men and lived under dominant world.

All the typical life came to an end her affectionate sister was reunited at the end after a long period of time. Walker has given us in *The Colour Purple* a brilliant Psychological developmental novel (dedicated "To the spirit; without whose assistance/Neither this book/Nor I/would have been/written":Walker has "listened with the- third ear"- her own unconsciousness).Celie's fictive narrative voice, that "speaks" to us though mute and that is never "heard" by those To whom she writes, transcends the limitations of the novel :as Victim and survivor, Celie attests to the importance of "good- Enough mothering" in the early years and to the healing power of human relationships.(12-37) When Africans were enslaved by Americans,they were denied to educate,they doesn't permit to speak their native language.Their freedom were ceized by Americans likewise where Celie is enforced into calm by Alfonso,she engages herself in writing letters and communicate with her readers.Even though Celie was torchered by her husband,she runs her own business by making pants.It was the best example of courage and hardwork.She didn't lose her hope.Celie find a better companion with Shug. She followed Shug's way of living for her own laws. After meeting Shug Celie got self confidence and stoped trusting men. When Shug was not well she cared her well and nurses with love until Shug back to health. They both loved each other, at the time of painful situations. At the end of the plot they both joined in forces. Celie is portrayed different in this Novel, she learned herself to balance all the circumstances. Marginalisation is discussed deeply by Walker in *The Colour Purple* with Celie's emancipation from male domination.

Walker wrote Meridian at the time when many black people were disobeying nonviolence and civil rights movement. Many critics interrupted Walker's work as suggestive of that the rebellion never addressed the misery of women.(3)Some critics consider that Walker employed Meridian to show her attitudes of Woman (4).Alice walker depicts Celie's practice of domination in a male dominated society, her sexual cruelty by her father and husband and how she productively moves toward up from surrender and repression to a self recognition and so accomplishing entire freedom. *The Colour Purple* resist of black women in America.

Alice Walker has expected her women as fatalities of violence and she ventures a victorious transform from a sufferer to a victorious women. Women are cruelly exploited and measured as meager objects planned only for male sexual fulfillment. Celie's world was one of dread, hopelessness, anxiety and aloneness, silent and terrible suffering, Colourless dark and with no ray of hope or sunshine.

From the very first chapter onwards Walker portrays a world of oppression and abuse of black girls and women. Walker tells story in the form of letters. Celie's attitude about herself and about god is clearly visible through the letters which she writes to God to help her to survive the spiritual emotional and physical abuse she suffers at the hands of her step father. The experiences of the black female leading role, Celie are obtainable through her association to God.

Through her letters to God Celie the fourteen year old girl narrates her first experience of sexism, her father sexually abusing her. Male dominance is always considered as a norm in such a society where Celie is abused. She is made to suffer by the man who she had for long believed to be her father. Her father's words, "She ain't fresh tho, but I aspect you know that. She stained. Twice..." (9), surprises the readers.

The horrendous account of the sexual brutality portrayed on the first page of the novel shows an areocentric culture which sees women as meager objects for sexual satisfaction. Her stepfather denies her the right for education, rapes her repeatedly and shatters her confidence. She is considered as ugly, dump and good for nothing. To save Nettie from an unpleasant relation she even becomes the wife of Mr. Albert.

She wants to protect her sister from her father's clutches and wants her to study and flee from the world of violence and domination. The feminine characters in the novel symbolize the collective perception of black women, the terror, pain and misery, their experiences, fortitude and hopes. Women in general are conditioned to a fearful reticence in their performance and being black intensifies it.

As a close equivalent to the mistreated black women the land too is refined to the severe in order to take greatest possessions out of it. The felling of trees, like traditional massive mahogany trees and the devastation of the forest divulge how the land, that was forced to recline flat and exposed as the palm of his hand. (153). Man morals nature or land only so far he can advantage out of it. So is the container with woman.

Celie is vulnerable and debilitated and not in a position to share her emotions and injury to another other than God. Her books manage the life of African Americans with a unique accentuation on the dark ladies' life. The dark ladies' life is an adventure from feebleness to the condition of strengthening and self acknowledgment and self acknowledgment.

In spite of the fact that Celie is considered as terrible and dull apparently, she has an inward quality which enables her to shield her sister from shades of malice that she has encountered. Celie's association with Shug Avery, a sure, glamourous, striking and wonderful ladies and the admirer of her significant other improves her attention to self, which enhanced her and empowered her to have better confidence in herself, and a fearlessness to confront the abominations and to express her emotions. A bond creates between them.

Celie's lesbian association with her helped them to be alright with their body and feel cherished. Ladies picking up quality through ladies is plainly delineated in *The Colour Purple*. She endures racial and sexual orientation separation. Yet works for the improvement of her kin and devotes herself completely to the work.

Ladies in *The Colour Purple* are abused, corrupted to the level of unimportant questions by men. Yet at the same time they with the assistance of other ladies can beat the mistreatment leveled upon them. The illustration of aggregate exertion and sisterhood is plainly depicted. Celie draws quality from it and encourages other ladies to increase internal quality.

With the assistance of other ladies she begins sewing garments and in this way figures out how to deal with her own particular life. The imagery of shading is extremely very much utilized as a part of the novel. Albert dependably demands Celie to wear dark Coloured or naval force blue shaded dresses which propose abuse and never enabled her to wear red or purple, those hues which remains for bliss. Later on Celie reasserts her own particular distinction and loves and designs her stay with purple.

Mistreatment has been an issue that has influenced human life for quite a while. A general public in light of collaboration and adjust as opposed to strength and chain of importance is fundamental for survival on this planet and tries to end all types of abuse. Walker recommends the representation of sisterhood and aggregate exertion and says that the endeavors made by man to oppress ladies can be halted by the unified endeavors of ladies themselves.

Celie step by step finds the power and delight of her own soul, liberating her from her past, rejoining her with those she cherishes by voicing against male centric request and accordingly accomplishes a self-sufficient state. In spite of everything ladies can raise their voice against shameful acts and recapture their internal quality and self hood. Alice Walker in the novel is therefore distracted with the survival entire of her kin and in investigating the abuses, the madnesses, the loyalties and the triumphs of dark ladies.

The Colour Purple by Alice Walker won her the Pulitzer prize and the American Book Award in 1983, for making an intense dark freed lady character in Celie who prevails during the time spent survival both at the level of self and group seriously with regards to the supremacist, sexist and classist society of America. The novel accounts the life of the dark young lady Celie who notwithstanding destitution, absence of education, and physical and additionally mental misuse, rises above her situation through mindfulness, and endeavors to scale the inconspicuous and warm measurements of womanish awareness.

Walker discloses to Celie's story as letters initially kept in touch with God and later to her sister Nettie. Celie, keeps in touch with God to help her to survive the profound, enthusiastic and physical mishandle she endures because of her dad (step father). In this manner, she starts her trip from weakness to the condition of full strengthening and from self-refusal to self-acknowledgment.

A Womanist Alice Walker calls herself 'womanist'. It is the term she authored to express the far reaching setting of Black Feminism. To her, 'womanist' is "a lady who acknowledges and favors ladies' way of life and lady's quality" (Culture, The Literature of the United States, 394). Advance she clarifies 'womanist association with "women's activist" by playing upon the title of her Pulitzer prize novel *The Colour Purple*: "Womanist is to women's activist as purple to lavender" (395), in this way concentrating on the shading measurement of Black woman's rights. Being a womanist, Alice Walker is more inspired by champions than in saints.

However, men not truant in her novel, they are just auxiliary. This helped her to adequately recasting the introduction of darkness in America. In *The Colour Purple* (1982), Alice Walker is worried about dark life and articulation when all is said in done, and female exploitation in a basically man centric world specifically.

She concentrates on the advancement of female wholeness: the improvement of recognize and group in Celie; the focal character in *The Colour Purple,* Celie is introduced as casualty of racial and sexual persecution. She is assaulted by the man she accepts to be her dad and she is battered and mishandled in a cold marriage. In any case, Gray remarks she step by step figures out how to develop into being a lady and pick up fellowship (697). *The Colour Purple* is an account of Celie's survival and her self-improvement that Happen to be composed as a progression of letters. The letters are composed to God.

Celie keeps in touch with God since her progression father called Alphonso cautioned her not to advise anyone of what he did to her. "You better never tell anyone but rather God. It'd execute your mammy" (Walker 1), her dad cautions her. Celie's first letter to God uncovers how she is influenced casualty to sexual wants by her progression to father Alphonso when her wiped out mother doesn't react to his lewd gestures.

Alphonso speaks to man centric dark world in which ladies are subjected to sexual abuse. Quiet accommodation to men's lewd gestures is normal from ladies and they can't make a cry against men. Celie encounters torment as she is being attacked by her dad. When she cries, her dad begins stifling her and says, "You better quiets down and got accustomed to it" (2). She is constrained upon parenthood; however she is uninformed of it.

She is a mother needing kids, since Alphonso removed her children from her. He might want Celie to look better than average after she brings forth two children. He looks in Celie for a substitute for his wiped out spouse and really he has substituted her. Celie has experienced the sexual mistreatment, as well as rehashed beatings because of her dad.

He beats Celie for reasons unknown specifically; first he beats her for she winked at a kid in chapel and on the other event he beats her for 'dressing trampy'. In the two cases the explanations behind beatings are not legitimate. Celie's position in the novel is the dark ladies' position all in all. Dark men might be defrauded by bigotry; however sexism enables them to go about as exploiters and oppressors of [black] ladies (Ranveer, Black Feminists Consciousness 17).

Alice Walker is one of those pioneers who celebrate womanhood in their writings. She calls herself a "womanist"; in her opinion, expresses woman's concerns better than feminism. It appreciates and prefers "women's culture, women's emotional flexibility, and women's strength" (1983 : xi).

In the fictional world of Walker, woman is no longer subservient to man, but rather struggles against her patriarchal culture and its institution to define her individual identity. Walker destroys, or subverts the old literary myths which are for heroes and creates new images of women in her novels. As a womanist she is concerned with the liberation of all womankinds from the psychology of oppression.

But as a black womanist writer she is more "committed to exploring the oppression, the insanities, the loyalties, and the triumphs of black woman" (Walker 1973 interviews with the black writes, 1973: 192). Walker clearly shows that they are victims of both racism and sexism in the American society and the same time seeks to transform them into emergent black women.

This note attempts to examine how Meridian, one of her most celebrated novels, reflects her strong belief in the black womanist tenets. It tells the story of the black woman in a period of transition, the story of a coming to consciousness and a subsequent development of self and search for authenticity. Oppression has been an issue that has affected human life for a very long time.

A society based on cooperation and balance rather than dominance and hierarchy is necessary for survival on this planet and seeks to end all forms of oppression. Walker suggests the metaphor of sisterhood and collective effort and says that the efforts made by man to subjugate women can be stopped by the united efforts of women themselves.

Celie gradually discovers the power and joy of her own spirit, freeing her from her past; reuniting her with those she loves by voicing against patriarchal order and thereby attains an autonomous state. Despite everything women are able to raise their voice against injustices and regain their inner strength and self hood. Alice Walker in the novel is thus preoccupied with the survival whole of her people and in exploring the oppressions, the insanities, the loyalties and the triumphs of black women. The present study deals with the discourse of womanism in the novels of Alice Walker.

Alice Walker, as an African American writer, has a great place in the African American literary field. She has contributed poetry, stories, essay collections, non-fictional work and novels to African American literature. She is also honoured with the Pulitzer Prize for her novel *The Colour Purple*. Her novels, in relation to discourse of womanism, are studied in this thesis.

The methods of descriptions and analysis are used for the study. In this study different aspects of the novels of Alice Walker, such as social contexts in the novels, cultural aspects in the novels, language, racism, sexism, struggle for self, survival and wholeness, the black art and womanist maternity are studied.

With the help of descriptive and analytical methods, the present work studies the discourse of womanism in all the novels of Alice Walker. All the aspects of womanism, such as behaviour of the characters, language of them, struggle, love, universalism and the relationships of the protagonists of all novels are discussed in this research. The importance of womanist movement, in relation to survival and wholeness of entire people, is also discussed.

As womanism focuses on political activities and struggle against racism, sexism, classism and oppression, all the female protagonists of the novels of Alice Walker are described in the light of womanism, The present study has its own pedagogical and social significance as Alice Walker has a great place in the field of African American literature. She is the first African American woman writer to win the Pulitzer Prize for literature.

A number of books by Alice Walker are the parts of Bachelor and Master Degree syllabi in different universities worldwide. In this relation the present research work is helpful for the students who undertake the study of Alice Walker's work. They may understand Alice Walker as a writer, her concept of womanism, the place of African American community in America, socio-political and economic status of African American males and females in America and the culture of this community.

They may come to know about certain inhuman practices, such as scarification and female genital mutilation, are prevailing in some tribes. The learners may also know about the African American women who are noticeably absent from American literature. Alice Walker has portrayed the women protagonists, who are the representatives of different layers of the African American community, through her novels.

She also has discussed a variety of issues like racism, sexism, oppression and socio-economic injustice with the help of her novels. These issues may work as areas of research in relation to new research students. Along with the pedagogical significance this study also has a social significance. There is a discussion of various social, political and economic aspects of African American community.

This discussion is helpful for the modern society in relation to acceptance and understanding of black women as a significant part of the society. The readers may understand the need of treating women as subjects rather than objects. The women of modern era will come to know the ways to fight against the exploitation and oppression.

The present study tries to make the new generations know the aspects of heritage of the Southern black community in America. The traditional customs as well as social and cultural values of the African Americans are carried to new generations. This knowledge is helpful to change the views of concerned people about women and it is also supportive for universalism, survival and wholeness.

Meridian (1976) is about a black woman Meridian Hill, who involves herself in civil rights movement with herself interest. The plot express he relationship she fails and her efforts to support the civil rights movement. Her relationship with Truman Held leads to teenage pregnancy, Truman becomes far more attached to her longs for stating a new life with her, Later he started loving a white woman named Lynne Rabinowitz, who is also involved in civil rights movement.

Truman is haunted by thoughts of his aggressive exploitation and he surrounds himself with pictures of Meridian, with paintings and sculptures of the Southern African-American women. By being pricked by his conscience, by being haunted by his crime of his exploitation, Truman makes himself accountable and thereby owns responsibility to a certain extent for his exploitation. He cannot "just walk away" from his crimes. As a teen Meridian does not have knowledge about sex, which results in teenage pregnancy. She is also sends out of school. She feels indifferent at best. Meridian's mother denies her interest with radical political activities. When Meridian fortunately offered a scholarship to Saxon College, she feels embarrassed and happy. Later Meridian's health condition worsens, losing her sight and become unconsciousness. Miss.Winters, one of Saxon's few black instructors, nurses her back to health. Walker argues about individuals overcome obstacles and define their characters. Meridian features earlier examples of strong female role models.(1) Meridian fought for injustice ,registering people to vote, indulge herself in civil rights movement. When Truman marries Lynne, ajewish exchange student. This makes Meridian get more anger on whites. Later Truman and Lynne had a daughter, named Camara. Five years later Camara Is beaten to death in a hate crime.

Meridian visits Newyork to comfort Truman and Lynne in their grief. This made Truman joins Meridian in a group with poor black families. She is working through her conflicts with violence and justice. Black feminist critics have focused on the struggle which originates from adolescence to maturity. Her quest for identity makes her indulge in civil rights movement. Walker focus on the racial experiences in African-American and womanist world is concerned of black women who were deeply alienated by the dominant white culture. As Karen Stein writes: ....the novel points out that the civil rights Movement often reflected the Oppressiveness of patriarchal capitalism.

Activists merely turned political rhetoric to their own ends while continuing to repress spontaneous individuality. To overcome this destructiveness, Walker reaches for a new definition of revolution. Her hope for a new society inheres political change, as well as personal transformation.(Stein 66) Meridian is considered as the protagonist of this novel whose existence presents a problem that will be solved only by her death.

Meridian undergone painful situation when she lost her child and longing for motherhood. She played a vital role personal sacrifice during civil rights movements as regarded as her best work depicted in this novel. The novel depicts important female characters. Meridian's mother is regarded as a religious woman and hatred nature who fails to show her love on her own daughter Meridian. Her mother fails to teach her about the caution of sex, Instead always she used to shout at her daughter. This becomes a hatredness towards her mother. She is the only child who left isolated in her family. Lynne, a Jewish civil rights worker, who marries Truman is already a lover of Meridian and impregnated her. The novel portrays the post life of Meridian and history of south. The novel is titled with the same name of the protagonist Meridian. Meridian is physically and psychologically abused. She didn't lose her will power. She protests for her identity and empowerment of women. When she is young, she is innocent kind and lovely, the childhood of Meridian is pleasant when she reached her adolescence she faces many problems throughout her life. She learns the limitations of her life after become motherhood.

Meridian's upbringing by her mother makes her emotionally starched shut, since her mother has refused her any knowledge of sex and Meridian's initiation to sex becomes a violent affair when she gets molested in a local funeral home. This experience of initiation to sex through horror of violence makes Meridian a woman who cannot enjoy having sex with men. Pifer has mentioned that while everyone thinks of Meridian as a "young wife and mother" and as a "perfect woman"," she is in fact, nearly died" (77-88).

By refusing motherhood, by saying "no", Meridian "offends and loses her own mother, her family, and her community"(77-88) states Pifer, adding, "she stops living by others standards, learns to bloom for herself, as she must in order to survive, since her rebellious acts will alienate her from the rest of society"(77-88). The discussion on the oppressor-oppressed relationship in Meridian may be concluded using the words of Karen F.Stein: Exposing herself to the forces of violence and stepping forward to challenge injustice, she is close to death...In defining herself as an artist, Meridian determines her salvation. Her art, hard-won from personal struggle, will be life-giving, Not death dealing.

...In order to live, Meridian rejects the temptations of Conventional middle-class life, the conventional women's roles Of dutiful daughter, wife, mother, lover...In her refusal to Accept such modeling, Meridian contrasts with earlier fictional Women who..Willingly sacrifice themselves to their husbands Quests for perfection..From her repeated encounters with Death for perfection...From her repeated encounters with Death and deathliness, she gains the knowledge and strength to Achieve a new birth of self.(130-142) Meridian -The protagonist of this novel understands her role in life is the major theme of the novel. Her struggle gains senses of self reorganization and express her relationship to African Americans. Racism and segregation the interconnection of the past and present, the difficulty of idealism is portrayed in the novel.

Meridian fought for the growth of civil rights movement. She fought for the quest of identity, she always remembers her past life .She undergone a bitter experience from the young age. She was abused by the landlord, George Daxter by offering her candy and money. Everything had become a nightmare. But these incidents do not denied her to have a boy friend Eddie. She does not bother about the society to posse a boy friend. She was disrespected by everyone even by her mother and left alone with her boyfriend as pregnant. As a teenager she does not aware of having baby, who would change her lifestyle. She is not serious about her early pregnancy. She is inspired by her boyfriend's love and kindness. Even he is also not matured enough to take decisions.

They were not aware of the reality of life, that immature relationship will ends with detachment. Their love started to fade, thus their marital life ends in divorce. According to Meridian marriage is a "Sanctuary", something which has cut her off from the outer world.(M 62).Later Meridian's motherhood frightens her to brought up her son which pricks her and leading her to entertain thoughts of suicide. She was struck between her husband and baby. She was also like her mother who does not find no pleasure and joy in married life. Walker indicates that marriage is a private affair but it should not destruct at the middle, a growth of the family is in the hands of couple.

Meridian was indeed of child because she fears about single parenting and society. She feels suffocated to posse child during young age. She herself curses. She does not want to rear her child in a society where black children were not given importance. And they will be dominated by white people .Meridian had caught between the tradition and society. Finally she renounces her child and decides to study at Saxon College. Later she willingly involved in Civil rights movement. But her inner conscious was always pricking her. This became a stress to Meridian which results in her illness. She soon recovers from her illness and dedicated her life to participate in Civil rights movement.

She fought for the justice of people, especially black people. Her emotional state was converted into a courageous state. She discovers herself as bold woman and learns to survive. Her rebellious fought for her people have been succeeded. She is trapped between her carrier and her child. Meridian is a kind hearted woman, as she takes a wild child to home, cares her, feeds her takes her custody.

When the wild child was meet with an accident she feels distressed and hate the society especially when the president of Saxon college denied to use college chapel for the funeral service. Meridian also reveals the exalted concept of self-sacrifice. To Meridian, the only reason for self-sacrifice, should be for preserving another life."...she against whatever obstacles was to live it, and not to give up any particle of it without a fight to the death, preferable not her own".

Thus one finds that oppression makes Meridian more mellowed and more sympathetic, though she acts rebellious initially. She realises that she is responsible for her rebirth, by embracing the art form and making herself reborn through her artistic expressions.

Chapter III
CONCLUSION

The oppressor-oppressed relationship results in injustice, inequality and oppression of women. The oppression of women takes the form of abuse, violence and rape resulting in traumatic experiences. The oppression of women may also lead to unwanted pregnancies and painful abortions, as revealed in these novels.

Violence leaves a psychic scar on the oppressed, which turn leads to further violence and murder. The relationship also results in an identity crisis. The oppressed assuming the role of an oppressor becomes a hateful byproduct, as it happens in the case of Grange Coopeland and Brownfield. But certain people like Grange Coopeland on their women, who had once been oppressors on their women, redeem themselves, by transforming into a sustaining protector of the weak, while people like Brownfield remain incorrigible and selfish.

The oppression leads to rebellion on the part of Coopeland and Celie regain their self image, by their own effort, by realizing their potential and by realizing their creative artistic abilities. In Walker's novels she portrays the oppression of women as well as the oppression of black people. Thus, the study of the oppressor-oppressed relationship in the fiction of Alice Walker proves to be thought provoking and fascinating.

In short, the study shows Alice Walker's intention to champion as a writer the cause of the African-American women. It is a classic example of an intention assuming the shape of a determination. Walker's own words stand testimony to her determination: I am preoccupied with the spiritual survival whole, Of my people.

But beyond that, I am committed to the Exploring the oppressions, the insanities, the loyalties and the Triumphs of the black women. At the beginning of the novel, Celie is downtrodden and considered as a defeated women. African-American women were living pre-Civil Rights. Black women were caught under the control of white man. They are often considered as a victim of violent crimes.

Celie discovers her own vision of God, though she gained a bitter experience she gains some pride in her heritage. Walker portrays about the unladed love towards her sister even after thirty years, during her separation from the family of biological. The major theme which is discussed in this novel is sexual discrimination. According to Celie sex is a violence act. She is physically abused by men.

Until she meets an inspiring women named Shug. It is discovered in this novel that sexuality is not just getting from one gender to other gender, its all about the partners who loved each other. Women should not be used as a beast to get physical pleasure rather than to give with her willingness.

Most probably women face many consequences to survive in the world, especially black women. Women are being dominated by men, women may also have desires, and they also have wishes. But men do not allow them to go accordingly. They underwent painful and pathetic life. Especially black women fight against sexual discrimination.

They are treated as slaves material basis of exploitation were considered as the highlights among black. Afro-American women were oppressed triply. They were economically under priviledged. They are forced to live a materialistic life. They underwent stress-related disease because they were mentally and physically, lack their energy.

Female character in *The Colour Purple* are trying to acquire freedom, they struggle for equal rights. Women were not aware of the society, they should protest for their equality, but they failed to do so. They are devoted and loyal towards the male members of their family. Because of this they gain much experience physically and emotionally.

Women should not give space to men. They have to be serious about their situation and should not share their experiences of inferior position towards other women. For instance if we take the character Celie in colour purple we can describe her as a timid girl. She is subjected to abuse by he own father .She is invisible and posses silence throughout the novel not only her step father even she has struggled from her husband.

Celie realized the seriousness of her situation only after the conversation with Shug. Women should go against the will of men but here Celie failed to protect for her freedom. She lacks her confidence, she is considered as coward woman. Celie got relief with the companion of Shug Avery who is considered as her role model. Shug teaches her to raise her voice against male domination.

Later on Celie is transformed into a self-confident and self-actualization woman. Celie's husband finally realised his mistake that he have treated his wife very badly and he regretted it later on he is influenced by the woman and determined himself to change his thoughts and he have started to treat woman equally.

This effects that it is to be proved much of the women is binding together and their impact will be able to change men. Third life of grange Copeland gives a realistic glimpse into life as a black man in the early to mid twentieth century. The impact, which slavery and racism, had on the real lives. Walker's imagination brings in the masterful way.

Men were so angry at their unfair position in society that they take it out on their wives and children and then in turn blame it on their treatment at the hand of white people. Grange family is miserable, poor existence with Grange barely acknowledges his son and frittering away what little money they have on booze, gambling and women.

The Oppressor-oppressed relationship causes a sort of blindness, making people either physiologically or psychologically blind to the passions, yearnings, sufferings and disappointments of their fellow men and women. Walker's fiction reveals the psychological blindness of men to recognize women. The women are ill-treated to such an extent that some of them are forced to commit suicide, while others are murdered in cold blood.

Their blindness forces the women to lose their identity. Likewise in Meridian realizes her life and concluded that the battle is won in small ways such as supporting blacks. African- American women are being abused right from their childhood. Inhuman acts such as sexual violence and the physiological and psychological effects caused by unwanted pregnancy and the resultant trauma caused by any one or a combination of these experiences on the oppressed women also find eloquent expressions in these writers. These writers have suggested the ways also for ending this violence and oppression by indicating that the possible solution must come from within, by realizing their role and responsibility. Alice Walker suggests indirectly in her Meridian, the Gandhian principles of Non-violence and

Noncooperation may deliver the goods, in their attainment of equality and justice, the pinnacle of their Civil Rights Movements. Meridian's quest is for personal space where she can define herself as she chooses to. She finished her journey of self identifying and extends herself image. Hence she was succeeded in evolving a new self. Meridian's bitter experiences made her to recognize herself. She had fulfilled her mission in civil rights movements. At the end of the plot she flourishes, she became strengthened and awakened in which the discovery made her to shine.

The blindness of the oppressor in turn leads to the problem of the loss of identity of the oppressed. The African-American youth wandering in the street feel frustrated and rootless. Their individuality and identity is lost in wilderness. The oppressive conditions and the effects of oppression lead the oppressed to a realization that the solution has to be derived from within, this realization attained through experiences of frustration, anger, violence and death.

Most of the protagonists realize that they have been ultimately responsible for their actions and they cannot escape from the after-effects. This sense of owing responsibility leads to further realization that the ultimate solution has to come from within. The experience and realization paves the way of finding the solution to the problems caused by oppression that the deliverance for the oppressed must come from within and that one form of violence-oppression-can never be erased with other forms of violence.

It is equally true to note that the American scene today is not what it used to be a hundred years earlier and one can say that such an attitudinal change has been brought about by the conscientious writings of novelists. A study of women oppressor relationship in the context of caste conflicts in India, offers a rich and thought provoking field. The frustration of the women oppressor is expressed in this dissertation.

9 798887 334752

Printed by Libri Plureos GmbH in Hamburg,
Germany